MR. MESSY

by Roger Hargreaves

D0169679

Mr Messy was the messiest person you've ever met in your whole life.

He looked messy because he was messy, in everything he did.

You could always tell where Mr Messy had been because he left a trail of messy fingerprints wherever he'd been.

Oh yes, Mr Messy was messy by name, messy by nature!

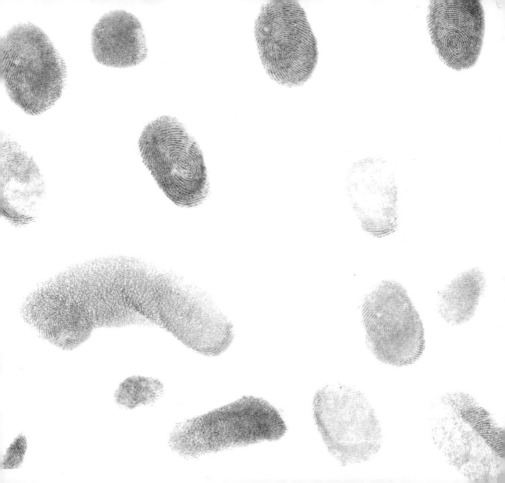

Mr Messy lived in a particularly messy looking house.

The paint was peeling.

The windows were broken.

There were tiles missing from the roof.

The flower beds were overgrown with weeds.

The garden gate was off its hinges.

And had Mr Messy cut the grass in his garden lately?

He had not!

One morning, Mr Messy woke up in his messy bed, yawned, scratched, got up, cleaned his teeth (leaving the top off the toothpaste), had his breakfast (spilling cornflakes all over the floor), and then set out for a walk (tripping over a brush he'd left lying in the garden two weeks before).

There was a wood behind Mr Messy's messy house with the messy garden, and that's where he went for his walk.

It was a particularly large wood with lots and lots of trees and it took Mr Messy a long time to walk through it. But he didn't really mind because he felt like walking that morning.

So he walked and walked right through the wood until he came to the other side.

And do you know what he found on the other side of the wood?

Mr Messy found the neatest, prettiest looking little cottage that he had ever seen.

It had a lovely little garden with a stream running through the middle of it.

There was a man in the garden, clipping the hedge.

He looked up as Mr Messy approached.

"Good morning! I'm Mr Messy!" said Mr Messy.

"I can see that," replied the man looking him up and down. "I'm Mr Tidy."

"And I'm Mr Neat," said another man, appearing out of the house.

"Tidy and Neat," said Mr Tidy.

"Neat and Tidy," said Mr Neat.

"We're in business together," explained Mr Tidy. "And the people who own this house have asked us to do some work for them."

"What sort of work?" asked Mr Messy.

"Oh, we make things nice and neat," said Mr Neat.

"Tidy things up," added Mr Tidy.

"Perhaps we could come along and do some work for you?" said Mr Neat looking at Mr Messy, who was looking even messier than usual that particular morning.

"But, I don't want things neat and tidy," said Mr Messy looking downright miserable at the thought of it.

"Nonsense!" said Mr Tidy.

"Fiddlesticks!" said Mr Neat.

"But," said Mr Messy.

"Come along," said Mr Neat.

"Off we go," said Mr Tidy.

"But, but . . . " said Mr Messy.

"But nothing," said Mr Neat, and bundling him into their van, which was parked behind the house, off they went to Mr Messy's house at the other side of the wood.

"Good heavens!" said Mr Neat when he saw where Mr Messy lived.

"Good gracious!" added Mr Tidy.

"This is the messiest house I have ever seen in all my born days," they both said together at the same time.

"Better do something about it," said Mr Neat.

And before Mr Messy could open his mouth, the two of them were rushing here and there about Mr Messy's house.

Mr Neat hoed

and mowed

and pruned

and snipped

and clipped

and cleared

and dug

and made the garden look neater than it had ever
looked before.

Mr Tidy cleaned

and primed

and rubbed

and painted

and mended

and made the outside of Mr Messy's house look tidier than it had ever looked before.

Then they both went inside the house.

"Good heavens!" said Mr Neat for the second time that morning.

"Good gracious!" said Mr Tidy for the second time that morning.

And then they set about cleaning the house from top to bottom.

They brushed and swept and polished and scrubbed and made the inside of the house look neater and tidier than it had ever looked before.

"There we are," said Mr Tidy.

"All finished," said Mr Neat.

"Tidy and neat," said Mr Tidy.

"Neat and tidy," said Mr Neat.

Mr Messy just didn't know what to say.

Then they both looked at Mr Messy.

"Are you thinking what I'm thinking?" Mr Neat said to Mr Tidy.

"Precisely," replied Mr Tidy.

"What we're both thinking," they said together to Mr Messy, "is that you look much too messy to live in a neat and tidy house like this!"

"But . . . " said Mr Messy.

But whatever Mr Messy said was no use, and Mr Neat and Mr Tidy whisked him off to the bathroom upstairs.

It had been the messiest room in the house, but now of course it was neat as a new pin.

Then Mr Neat got hold of one of Mr Messy's arms, and Mr Tidy got hold of the other arm, and they picked him up and put him straight into the bath.

Mr Messy wasn't used to having baths!

Mr Neat and Mr Tidy washed
                    and brushed
                    and cleaned
                    and scrubbed
                    and combed Mr Messy until
he didn't look like Mr Messy at all.

In fact he looked the opposite of messy!

He looked at himself in the mirror.

"You know what I'm going to have to do now?" he
said in a rather fierce voice.

Mr Neat and Mr Tidy looked worried.

"What are you going to have to do?" they asked Mr Messy.

"I'm going to have to change my name!" said Mr Messy.

And then he chuckled.

And Mr Neat and Mr Tidy chuckled.

And then Mr Messy laughed.

And Mr Neat and Mr Tidy laughed.

And then they all laughed together, and became the best of friends.

And that really is the end of the story, except to say that if you're a messy sort of person you might have a visit from two people.

And you know what they are called, don't you?

3 Great Offers for MR.MEN Fans!

MR.MEN TOKEN

3 Sixteen Beautiful Fridge Magnets – any 2 for £2.00!
inc.P&P

They're very special collector's items!
Simply tick your first and second* choices from the list below
of any 2 characters!

1st Choice

- [ ] Mr. Happy
- [ ] Mr. Lazy
- [ ] Mr. Topsy-Turvy
- [ ] Mr. Bounce
- [ ] Mr. Bump
- [ ] Mr. Small
- [ ] Mr. Snow
- [ ] Mr. Wrong

- [ ] Mr. Daydream
- [ ] Mr. Tickle
- [ ] Mr. Greedy
- [ ] Mr. Funny
- [ ] Little Miss Giggles
- [ ] Little Miss Splendid
- [ ] Little Miss Naughty
- [ ] Little Miss Sunshine

2nd Choice

- [ ] Mr. Happy
- [ ] Mr. Lazy
- [ ] Mr. Topsy-Turvy
- [ ] Mr. Bounce
- [ ] Mr. Bump
- [ ] Mr. Small
- [ ] Mr. Snow
- [ ] Mr. Wrong

- [ ] Mr. Daydream
- [ ] Mr. Tickle
- [ ] Mr. Greedy
- [ ] Mr. Funny
- [ ] Little Miss Giggles
- [ ] Little Miss Splendid
- [ ] Little Miss Naughty
- [ ] Little Miss Sunshine

*Only in case your first choice is out of stock.

--- TO BE COMPLETED BY AN ADULT ---

**To apply for any of these great offers, ask an adult to complete the coupon below and send it with
the appropriate payment and tokens, if needed, to MR. MEN CLASSIC OFFER, PO BOX 715, HORSHAM RH12 5WG**

- [ ] Please send _____ Mr. Men Library case(s) and/or _____ Little Miss Library case(s) at £5.99 each inc P&P
- [ ] Please send a poster and door hanger as selected overleaf. I enclose six tokens plus a 50p coin for P&P
- [ ] Please send me _____ pair(s) of Mr. Men/Little Miss fridge magnets, as selected above at £2.00 inc P&P

Fan's Name _____

Address _____

_____ **Postcode** _____

Date of Birth _____

Name of Parent/Guardian _____

Total amount enclosed £_____

- [ ] **I enclose a cheque/postal order payable to Egmont Books Limited**
- [ ] **Please charge my MasterCard/Visa/Amex/Switch or Delta account** (delete as appropriate)

| | | | | | | | | | | | | | | | | Card Number

Expiry date ___/___   **Signature** _____

MR.MEN   LITTLE MISS
Mr. Men and Little Miss™ & ©Mrs. Roger Hargreaves

CUT ALONG DOTTED LINE AND RETURN THIS WHOLE PAGE